Little Blossom S

Pepper's New Bed

By Cecilia Minden

2 Gram looks at Pepper's bed.

Pepper's bed looks sad.

"We will get you a new bed," says Gram.

Gram and Pepper look
for a new bed.

"Do you like this one?"

Pepper shakes his head.

"Do you like this one?"

Pepper shakes his head.

"Do you like this one?"

Pepper nods his head.

"Look, Pepper, a new
bed for naps."

Pepper naps in his new bed.

Word List

sight words

a	head	Look	Pepper	this
and	his	looks	Pepper's	We
Do	like	new	says	you
for	look	one	shakes	

short a words	short e words	short i words	short o words
at	bed	in	nods
Gram	get	will	
naps			
sad			

Gram looks at Pepper's bed.

Pepper's bed looks sad.

"We will get you a new bed," says Gram.

Gram and Pepper look for a new bed.

"Do you like this one?"

Pepper shakes his head.

"Do you like this one?"

Pepper shakes his head.

"Do you like this one?"

Pepper nods his head.

"Look, Pepper, a new bed for naps."

Pepper naps in his new bed.

Published in the United States of America by Cherry Lake Publishing Group
Ann Arbor, Michigan
www.cherrylakepublishing.com

Illustrator: Becky Down

Cherry Blossom Press is an imprint of Cherry Lake Publishing Group.

Library of Congress Cataloging-in-Publication Data

Names: Minden, Cecilia, author. | Down, Becky, illustrator.
Title: Pepper's new bed / written by Cecilia Minden ; illustrated by Becky Down.

Description: Ann Arbor, Michigan : Cherry Lake Publishing, 2021. | Series:
   Little blossom stories | Audience: Grades K-1. | Summary: "Gram shops
   for a new bed for Pepper. Will Gram find Pepper a bed that is just
   right? This A-level story uses decodable text to raise confidence in
   early readers. The book uses a combination of sight words and
   short-vowel words in repetition to build recognition. Original
   illustrations help guide readers through the texts"– Provided by
   publisher.
Identifiers: LCCN 2020030337 (print) | LCCN 2020030338 (ebook) | ISBN
   9781534179653 (paperback) | ISBN 9781534180666 (pdf) | ISBN
   9781534182370 (ebook)
Subjects: LCSH: Readers (Primary)
Classification: LCC PE1119.2 .M56748 2021 (print) | LCC PE1119.2 (ebook)
   | DDC 428.6/2—dc23
LC record available at https://lccn.loc.gov/2020030337
LC ebook record available at https://lccn.loc.gov/2020030338

Printed in the United States of America

Cecilia Minden is the former director of the Language and Literacy Program at Harvard Graduate
School of Education. She earned her PhD in Reading Education at the University of Virginia. Dr.
Minden has written extensively for early readers. She is passionate about matching children to the
very book they need to improve their skills and progress to a deeper understanding of all the wonder
books can hold.

CHERRY BLOSSOM PRESS